Migrating Animals

Humpback Whales

B.J. Best

New York

Published in 2017 by Cavendish Square Publishing, LLC
243 5th Avenue, Suite 136, New York, NY 10016

Copyright © 2017 by Cavendish Square Publishing, LLC

First Edition

No part of this publication may be reproduced, stored in a retrieval system, or transmitted in any form or by any means—electronic, mechanical, photocopying, recording, or otherwise—without the prior permission of the copyright owner. Request for permission should be addressed to Permissions, Cavendish Square Publishing, 243 5th Avenue, Suite 136, New York, NY 10016. Tel (877) 980-4450; fax (877) 980-4454.

Website: cavendishsq.com

This publication represents the opinions and views of the author based on his or her personal experience, knowledge, and research. The information in this book serves as a general guide only. The author and publisher have used their best efforts in preparing this book and disclaim liability rising directly or indirectly from the use and application of this book.

CPSIA Compliance Information: Batch #CW17CSQ

All websites were available and accurate when this book was sent to press.

Library of Congress Cataloging-in-Publication Data

Names: Best, B.J.
Title: Humpback whales / B.J. Best.
Description: New York : Cavendish Square Publishing, 2017. | Series: Migrating animals | Includes index.
Identifiers: ISBN 9781502621108 (pbk.) | ISBN 9781502621122 (library bound) | ISBN 9781502621115 (6 pack) | ISBN 9781502621139 (ebook)
Subjects: LCSH: Humpback whale--Juvenile literature.
Classification: LCC QL737.C424 B47 2017 | DDC 599.5'25 --dc23

Editorial Director: David McNamara
Copy Editor: Nathan Heidelberger
Associate Art Director: Amy Greenan
Designer: Alan Sliwinski
Production Coordinator: Karol Szymczuk
Photo Research: J8 Media

The photographs in this book are used by permission and through the courtesy of: Cover Betty Wiley/Moment/Getty Images; p. 5 miblue5/iStock/Thinkstock.com; p. 7 Shane Gross/Shutterstock.com; p. 9 Karim Iliya/Barcroft Media via Getty Images; p. 10 MZPHOTO.CZ/Shutterstock.com; p. 12 John Tunney/Shutterstock.com; p. 15 Achimdiver/Shutterstock.com; p. 16 Joost van Uffelen/Shutterstock.com; p. 18 Tomas Kotouc/Shutterstock.com; p. 21 suefeldberg/iStock/Thinkstock.com.

Printed in the United States of America

Contents

How Humpback Whales Migrate **4**

New Words **22**

Index **23**

About the Author **24**

Humpback whales live all over the world.

Humpback whales are one of the largest animals.

They can be as long as a school bus!

7

Humpbacks **migrate**.

They can swim over 3,000 miles (4,800 kilometers).

In the summer, humpbacks are in cold water.

They eat lots of food.

Humpbacks eat **krill**.

They also eat small fish.

13

Humpbacks swim to warm water in the winter.

They do not eat.

They have babies.

15

A baby humpback is called a **calf**.

It weighs 2,000 pounds (900 kilograms) when it is born.

The whales will swim to cold water again.

They will eat there.

Humpbacks can **breach**.

They jump out of the water.

People love to watch whales!

21

New Words

breach (BREECH) To jump out of water.

calf (KAF) A baby whale.

krill (KRILL) An animal like a shrimp.

migrate (MY-grate) To travel far.

Index

babies, 14, 16

breach, 20

calf, 16

eat, 10, 12, 14, 18

krill, 12

migrate, 8

summer, 10

winter, 14

About the Author

B.J. Best lives in Wisconsin with his wife and son. He has written several other books for children. He has been whale-watching but did not see a whale.

About BOOKWORMS

Bookworms help independent readers gain reading confidence through high-frequency words, simple sentences, and strong picture/text support. Each book explores a concept that helps children relate what they read to the world they live in.